My Dear Children,

Before you read *A Tooth Fairy Named Mort*, I would like to tell you the backstory of how I met Mort and learned all the secrets of Fairyland. You see, the backstory is the story of what happened back before there was a story at all.

The Backstory of
A Tooth Fairy Named Mort

With the excitement of spring in the air, I headed out one Friday evening for a walk around the small lake near my home. I chose a trail leading to my favorite rock that towers over the water, where I can sit and watch the sun shining through the trees and reflecting upon the lake.

Perched high on the rock, I began to think about my week—what did I do well and what could I have done better? Did I take care of myself? Did I take time to help others? Did I give the gift of a smile to all who passed my way?

Deep in thought, I noticed little sparkles just over the top of the waves—at first only a few, then more began to appear. They stretched from the middle of the lake clear to the opposite bank. I wondered what they could be.

Spying a narrow deer trail close to the edge of the lake, I decided to explore. As I made my way down the path, the sparkles seemed to shift away from me. They kept moving, but so did I—even more slowly now, choosing every step carefully so as not to make a single crunch or rustle one leaf.

Gradually, I neared a place where the sparkles came clear to the shore. I crouched down, waited patiently, and held as still as my curious body could hold.

Have you ever had the feeling that someone was watching you, and when you turned, no one was there? That's the feeing I had. I turned, and I turned again, but no one was there. Yet the feeling remained. So, I sat perfectly still for two long minutes, then ever so slowly, like an owl, I turned just my head.

My eyes scanned the ground, the bushes, and the branches of the trees until finally, I saw her perched on the limb of an evergreen tree. Only inches high, with clothes made of petals, a crown of tiny flowers, and leaf-like wings, she was well camouflaged, sitting there in the tree. No wonder I hadn't seen her.

I rubbed my eyes, then opened them—she was still there! I was not imagining her! Gracefully, she spread her wings and flew toward me, landing on a flower right in front of me, and she began to talk in a voice as sweet and smooth as honey.

"I am the Tooth Fairy. My name is Mortina, and I have been watching you for many evenings as you walk around the lake. I believe you are the one Santa's elves, Quest and Shield, told me about. They said you understand fairies, elves, and magical things, and that you might be able to help me."

She tipped her head, and with a persuasive smile, she went on, "As you know, little ones everywhere pull their teeth and put them under their pillow for me, without knowing the reason I need each tooth. Last month, at our Spring Solstice Celebration, the fairies decided it was time to tell the children what happens to their teeth and the magic they bring to Fairyland."

Raising her delicate eyebrows, she asked, "May I take you to Fairyland and tell you my story?"

My mouth was unable to form a single word, so I nodded, took a deep breath, and began to smile when I realized—I was going to fly! Mort reached into a pouch hanging around her waist, then hovering over my head, she sprinkled fairy dust, and as it drifted down, it was like a gentle mist leaving tiny kisses all over my skin.

"We must go now," she said. "There is only a short window of time when we can come and go, and when the sun gets too low, our time is up."

Off we went across the lake, flying just between the top of the waves and the breeze coming out of the west. As our speed picked up, I noticed each sparkle was more than just a sparkle—it was another fairy coming or going—but from where I did not know. Suddenly the breeze gave a little lift, and POP! we disappeared from where we had been and reappeared on a sandy beach near a castle that only fairy magic could have created.

Making ourselves comfortable on a large piece of driftwood, Mortina began to tell me the story of this island that is home to fairies and other flying creatures you have never before imagined.

She described every colorful detail, then eagerly asked if I could make her story into a book to share with children around the world. Right away, I agreed, because I was sure you and others would love to hear all the secrets of Fairyland and the fairies' desperate need of one child's tooth.

With our agreement set and a little more fairy dust over my head, we swiftly flew back to where we had met. As we said good-bye,

Mortina asked me to meet her in this very spot every spring for a special fairy party. At that instant, she turned, flew off, and disappeared over the water, just as the sun sank below the horizon.

Quickly walking home as the day faded, I realized I had not spoken a word during the entire adventure. Soon, while sitting at my desk with pen and paper, the words came and would not stop. I wrote every magnificent detail so you could know about the Tooth Fairy, her important job, her friends, and her home on a fairy island. Turn the page to begin the story of *A Tooth Fairy Named Mort.*

This book is dedicated to those who fly on the wings of imagination to worlds beyond—where magic lives!

And to the children in my life who continually inspire me to take flight.

A Tooth Fairy Named Mort

By Sharon Thayer
Illustrations by Reuben McHugh
and Andrew Smith

If you could fly across the water,
just as the sun begins to set,
and slip between the top of the waves
and the breeze coming out of the west,
you would come to a lovely beach of sand,
right on the edge of Fairyland.

And if you sat there perfectly still,
the moon would rise and cast its spell,
as the fairy castle comes alive,
with every imaginable flying creature waking inside.

This castle is home to fairies and more,
flying in windows and gliding out doors,
flitting around, casting spells,
singing songs, and ringing bells.

Some large, some small, some short, and some tall.
Some of many colors, and some, no color at all.
Blue and yellow, purple and green,
so handsome, so beautiful,
and no two the same.

There are fairies who cook
and some who clean,
and flying dragons who fix machines.
One fairy's in charge of shining the stars.
One gathers sweet nectar
from near and far.

Ten dear little pixies sew glorious gowns,
from spider webs and silky down.
The fastest fairy of all gathers the sun's rays,
to spread through the castle
on dark gloomy days.

Each has a job they love to do,
pixies, flying dragons, and Fairy Godmothers, too.
Together they do chores of every sort . . .
. . . especially the little Tooth Fairy named Mort.

Mortina, or Mort for short,
is an adventurous fairy—the tomboy sort.
Some days she tires of fluttering wings,
of fairy dust and magical things.

She'd rather dart through the forest and fly through the skies,
catching bright crystals and blue dragonflies.
But, like all her Fairyland friends,
she has a job she must do.
Her work assures their flying never ends,
and she's counting on you to help her through.

One pearly white tooth each day is required,
she must find at least one, even when she is tired.
For inside the tooth of every child,
is a magical power that lives for a while.
The brighter the tooth, the more magic it holds,
so brush every day, the way you've been told.

One morning you'll wake, to find one baby tooth,
is ever so slightly, a little bit loose.
So, you pull with your fingers and push with your tongue,
as the challenge to extract it has just begun.
It may take many tugs or fall out in your cup,
no reason to worry—you're growing up!
You'll hear it again and again as you grow,
to make room for the new, let go of the old.

Mort will come for your tooth, but it wouldn't be right,
to not leave you a present—it's only polite.
So, with your tooth tucked safely beneath your pillow,
she searches your neighborhood—high and low.
Under and over and in between,
she looks for a sparkle,
she looks for a sheen,
of coins or trinkets somewhere around,
and perhaps tonight, there is more to be found.

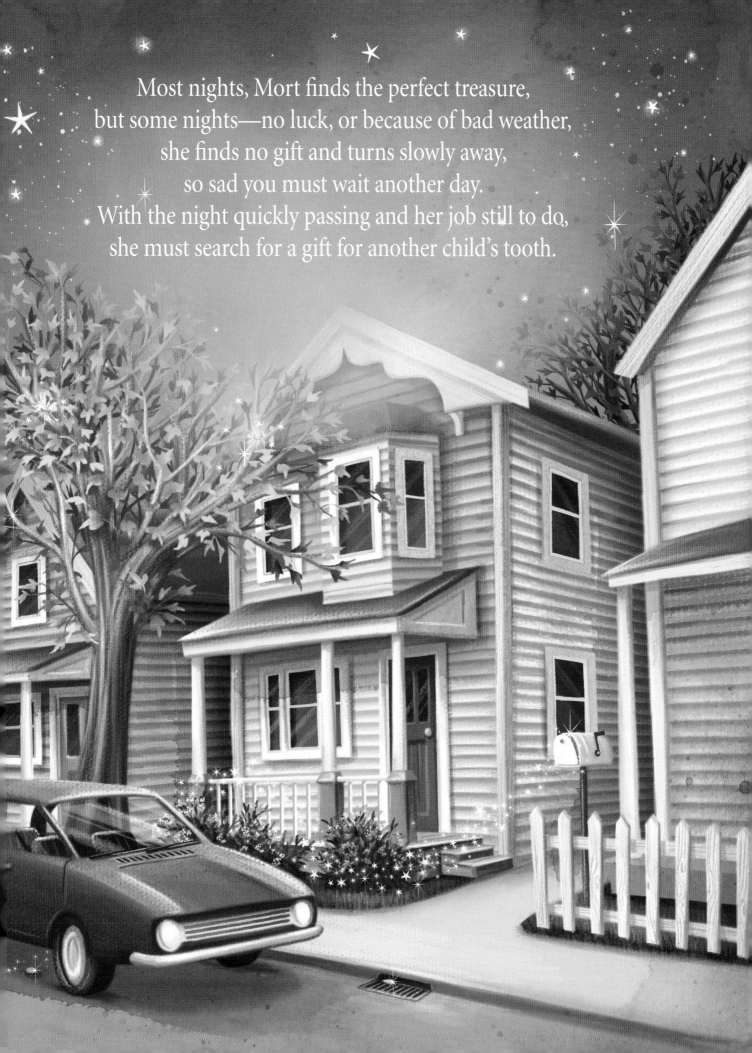

Most nights, Mort finds the perfect treasure,
but some nights—no luck, or because of bad weather,
she finds no gift and turns slowly away,
so sad you must wait another day.
With the night quickly passing and her job still to do,
she must search for a gift for another child's tooth.

Early tomorrow, her quest for your gift begins once more,
as around the earth for you she'll soar.
When a treasure is found—large or small,
swiftly she flies to the best tooth of all.

Guided by dreams and a secret wish,
Mort comes to your window and beneath it she slips,
with money or other splendid things,
a heavy load carried by dainty wings.

Mort's hunger grows through the long dark night,
so please, to help her through this magical flight,
leave nuts, or berries, or something green,
next to your window, before you drift off to dream.
Arriving exhausted, she'll sit for a while,
enjoying her treat, after flying for miles.

Soon energized, she glides to your pillow,
where she pushes, twists, and wiggles,
until she finds the tooth you've cared for each day,
bright and shiny in every way.
Mort places it safely, deep in her pack,
leaves a gift, whispers, "thank you," then turns to head back.

The night's nearly over, her job is done.
Now she hurries home, racing the sun.
Just in time, before dawn she lands,
in a circle of friends waiting on the sand.
Mort holds high the tooth upon her return,
the cherished one, for which they yearn.

Gregor, the Grinder Fairy, who sits alone,
places your tooth against his stone.
As he pumps the wheel, it spins and whines,
turning your tooth to dust as he grinds.

Then, with a kiss from the first sparkling ray of morning sun,
the dust comes magically undone,
releasing the power of contagious laughter,
the spirit of a child, bringing magic forever after.
Mort fills her pouch with this glittering dust,
from the most precious tooth that ever was.

Slowly rising, above her friends she flies around,
sprinkling fairy dust, and as it floats down,
glittering through the misty air,
it settles upon fairy cheeks and silken hair.

Ever so slowly, magnificent wings begin to unfold,
filling the morning with beauty untold.
As they stretch and their colors come alive,
Mort reaches in her bag to find one last sparkle inside.

While all heads turn toward the fading night,
Mort tosses it up with all her might.
Swiftly it soars to join the stars,
a brand-new twinkling, now seen from afar.

It shines to remind you, that as you grew,
you let go of the old to wait for the new,
and with your shining tooth,
you gave the magical gift of flight
to every winged creature in Fairyland
this fairy night.

Now, each spring on a particular evening when a gentle breeze is coming out of the west, I head down the narrow trail by the lake to find our special spot. Once there, I wait for the sparkles over the lake to POP! bringing not just Mortina but other fairy friends carrying freshly baked treats and sweet nectar for our annual celebration.

A tall, handsome fairy, wearing a hat fit for a king, pulls tiny cups from his backpack, and then other fairies pour sweet nectar into the cups as they chatter excitedly. Together we hold our cups high and make a toast.

"To the children—our friends,
who let go as they grow,
so our magic never ends."

Later, at my workshop, I carefully pack each book to ship to children in homes around the world. When my work is done, I'm off on a new adventure to enjoy the delicate beauty and stunning power of nature surrounding me as I hunt for another story to tell you.

I hope to see you out there, too, hiking, biking, or kayaking across a sparkling lake. And through your adventures, remember to give the gift of a smile to everyone along your path and always keep both eyes open—because you never know what you might find around the next corner.

Never stop believing!
Ms. Sharon

A Tooth Fairy Named Mort

First Edition 2018
10 9 8 7 6 5 4 3 2

Layout & Graphics - Jenny Hancey, Jenny@HanceyDesign.com
Editing - Sharon Roe, Sharon@SharonRoe.com

Carousel Publishing
15126 State Hwy. 110 S. Whitehouse, TX 75791
903-871-9872
cs@Carousel-Publishing.com
www.Carousel-Publishing.com

Library of Congress Cataloging-in-Publication Data
Thayer, Sharon C.

Summary: After hundreds of years of keeping the secrets, the Grand Fairy Council has ruled that
it is time to tell children about where the Tooth Fairy lives, why she needs their teeth, and why
she doesn't show up some nights.

This story, as it was told to Ms. Sharon by the Tooth Fairy herself, gives a glimpse into Fairyland
and unveils the truth of how children hold the power to continue fairy magic forever.

1. Tooth Fairy juvenile fiction 2. Fairies juvenile fiction 3. Children's juvenile fiction
4. Customs juvenile fiction 5. Traditions juvenile fiction

ISBN: 978-0-9766239-8-4
LCCN: 2018934816

Printed in the United States.

Carousel
PUBLISHING